Whoop for Joy

A Christmas Wish

By Jane Briggs-Bunting

Illustrations by Jon Buechel

Black River Trading Company
     P.O. Box 7
     Oxford, Michigan 48371
     810/628-2986

Printed in the United State of America by Worzalla Printers/Binders

Library of Congress Cataloguing-in-Publication Data
Briggs-Bunting, Jane, 1950-
     Whoop for Joy A Christmas Wish / by Jane Briggs-Bunting,
     Illustrations by Jon Buechel
     32 pages
     Summary: Children's story about a horse and a lonely little girl.

     ISBN 0-9649083-0-1
     1. Children's writing, American.
     95-95152

To my parents,
David and Isabelle Briggs,
and, of course,
Whoop for Joy

Beth knew without a doubt that nothing would ever be right again. The troubles started just after the winter break at school.

Dad got a new job at work which meant they all had to move to another state. Though she and Mom waited until school was over, she knew for the last six months that she'd never see Jennie, her best friend in the whole world, again. She'd be starting sixth grade absolutely friendless.

Then there was the baby. Mom cried a little. Dad did, too. Mom told her it was a surprise they'd stopped hoping for. Wasn't she lucky? Wasn't it wonderful? She was going to be a big sister. She'd have a playmate. She was 11, for goodness sakes. She'd have nothing in common with a crying, gurgling, little baby.

She knew about younger brothers and sisters. Most of her friends had them. The truth is, they were usually brats. Taking your stuff, playing with your toys, breaking them, always getting all the attention for doing silly things that, if you did them, you'd just get yelled at.

Being an older sister wasn't so great either. It meant you had to watch the baby, you were responsible for them. If it cried, the first question out of anyone's mouth was what happened, like it was your fault.

Mom got fatter and fatter. She was always tired and crabby. She couldn't do things like she used to—like field a ball or even walk very well.

Dad was gone all week, but he'd come home most weekends. A couple of weekends they went to Michigan to stay with him in his apartment. The three of them went house hunting. They had a list of things they wanted. Nobody asked her what she really wanted—to stay in Cleveland, where they were, with Jennie just two blocks away and at school everyday.

A couple of times she spent the weekend at Jennie's while her mother went to Michigan for even more house hunting.

Then they spent days and days and days packing. Clothes, toys, dishes, pans were swallowed up in boxes. There were so many boxes that Beth lost count of them.

When school was out, a big moving van with men came and hauled all the boxes, the beds, and the furniture into the truck. She said good-bye to Jennie and cried and cried. Then she drove with Mom on the freeway to Michigan, through a big city, then out to the country when they finally got off the freeway. They drove for what seemed a long time further, then turned down a long, bumpy road, up a two-track path, and there they were, at a house in the middle of nowhere!

There were no kids around. There were no houses around. But, Grandma was there to help out.

The van rumbled up a short while later, and men started carrying in their stuff. The adults sent her out "to explore."

Head down, fists clenched, her stomach in such a knot she thought she would burst, she headed down the driveway, quickly reversing direction when yet another car rumbled up the drive.

She started kicking pebbles furiously, so deep in her unhappiness she was unaware of anything until she was startled by an unfamiliar, deep-throated rumbling noise to her left. She looked over and saw the smooth satiny head of a horse, ears pricked towards her, leaning over the fence line watching. He whickered again, almost like he was saying "Hi!" to her.

Then he bobbed his head down and stretched his neck as far as he could under the fence to nibble a few blades of grass. He raised his head up again and leaned back over the

fence. She could almost see him pointing to a tall clump of grass just out of his reach.

She yanked a handful and held it towards him. He carefully snuffled her outstretched hand. Then he daintily nibbled the longest blades, pulling them gently out of her hand. When it was gone, he looked at her hopefully.

She started pulling clumps one after another, offering them to the horse. Slowly, they made their way down the fence line.

Oblivious to everything but the horse, she was startled when a woman's voice called out, "Hi, there. You must be Beth. I'm Ann. I see you've already made Whoop's acquaintance. He'll be your friend for life if you keep giving him grass."

Suddenly, Beth was embarrassed. "Was that all right? I know horses eat grass. He seemed to almost ask me for it."

The woman laughed. "It's perfectly okay. This sly fellow was probably taking advantage of you."

"I don't mind. . . . His name is Hoop?"

"Yes, Whoop for Joy, that's W-H-O-O-P. He's a good old boy. He's a retired racehorse that I trained for other types of riding. He's getting older now, so we just ride for pleasure. Do you know how to ride?"

"No, but I always wanted to learn."

"I think your folks were talking about riding lessons

for you at a stable up the road."

"Really?"

"Yes, your dad asked me about it when he was looking at the house. He said he had a daughter who loved horses, so he wanted to buy a house in the country so she could learn to ride. Does that make things seem a little better?"

Beth gave Ann a swift look, surprised she understood what Beth had been feeling.

"You know Whoop's lonely, too. I've got to work and can't spend as much time with him as I'd like to. We're next door neighbors. Maybe you'd like to come over and just visit with him sometimes. He's very gentle, and I'm sure he'd like you to feed him the grass that's just out of reach."

"You wouldn't mind?"

"Nope. What about you, Whoop?"

The tall bay gelding bobbed his head up and down.

"It's okay with Whoop, too. . . . I think someone's calling you."

Beth looked and saw her grandmother waving to her to come in. "I guess I've got to go. I'll see you later. Bye!" Beth rushed back to the house eager to tell her grandmother the wonderful news—they had a horse for a next door neighbor, and he wanted to be her friend.

All that summer, Beth would get up, eat her breakfast then hurry down the fence line where Whoop, his head

down grazing, seemed to watch for her. When she'd call his name, he'd look up, and walk, or sometimes trot, over to the fence line to see what treat she'd brought him. His favorites were apples and carrots.

Ann taught her how to groom him using curry combs and brushes, and to put on his pink, fuzzy fly screen to protect his eyes from the pesky summer flies. One really hot day, Ann showed her how to give him a bath.

Whoop loved a bath. When Beth would get the hose out, he'd come charging up, snorting and stand there perfectly still with his head raised waiting for her to squirt his chest.

Then he'd turn to his right, then his left, so the deliciously cool well water covered every inch of him from his neck down—he didn't like his head or face wet though, he would slurp water right from the hose sometimes.

When he had enough, he'd trot back to the corral, and with a grunt he'd lower himself down on his knees to roll in the dust. Ann told her that both the ancient Chinese and the Native American Indians could tell how smart a horse was by the way it rolled. Horses that could roll all the way over and all the way back were the smartest and bravest for hunting. Of course, that was exactly the way Whoop rolled because he was a smart horse.

Beth noticed other horses rolling after baths or just in

the dust on a hot day at the stable where she took her lessons. Many could only roll over to one side and then get up. Others couldn't get over at all. Only a very few could do what Whoop did. Horses were a lot like people, she decided. Some were smarter than others, and Whoop, in Beth's judgment, was definitely near genius!

As she became a better rider, on occasion Ann and Whoop would join her on a trail ride with one of the stable's mounts. When he was younger, Ann had ridden Whoop in horse shows. Whoop had a wall full of blue, red and green ribbons charting his many successes. But now, at 22, he was officially retired. Ann rarely jumped him except over a fallen log blocking a trail. Beth's fat stable pony could step over it, but Whoop would sometimes feel frisky and leap over it. Mainly they kept to a walk, which was just fine with Beth since she was still a beginner.

A couple of times, when Ann was too busy, Beth even got to ride Whoop on a long, leisurely trail walk.

When school started and the big yellow bus would rumble to a stop at the end of the drive, Beth would take a deep breath, swallow and climb aboard. The new school was different. She'd found no close friends like Jennie, and even the girls she'd met over the summer at the stables had their own friends. She was the outsider.

In the afternoons when the bus dropped her off, she

would run inside to greet her mother, change clothes, grab two apples and rush out the back door. Whoop would be waiting for her, head leaning over the fence, giving her his deep-throated rumbling greeting.

Finally, the new baby came. One night, Dad took Mom to the hospital. Beth went over to Ann's house until her grandmother arrived to put her to bed. The next day she met her new brother—tiny, red and wrinkled. She couldn't understand how any one could think that was "adorable"; now a baby horse would have been another thing entirely.

When the baby came home a day later, Beth swore she spent most of the time she was indoors tiptoeing around so she wouldn't wake him up. He had no such consideration for her, she thought, screaming his head off half the night when she was trying to sleep. Mom seemed never to have time for her. The baby always interrupted them when she was discussing her day with Mom or when Mom was helping her with homework. She shared all of this new misery with Whoop who would whicker in sympathy, playfully nudge her with his nose, and even play a horse version of tag.

The first time he'd done it, she'd been almost afraid. He came charging up to her, nudged her, wheeled around and trotted away, stopping a short way off, just looking at her. When she didn't do anything, he had snorted at her, trotted back to her, then raced off again. This time she did her own human version of a gallop after him. He took off with his tail up, neck arched, head tilted up in the air. She spent the next half hour or so chasing after him. He'd let her get almost close enough, then he'd race off again.

When she told Ann about it later, she learned the game was Whoop's own invention which Ann called "I'm going to get you." It was usually played with a halter, but Whoop now didn't even need that to get up a game.

Another favorite game was to flip water out of his trough. On a hot day, he'd stand there just splashing water by flinging his head down towards the trough, catching the water's surface with his lips and throwing his head up.

Sometimes on a sunny afternoon, Whoop would be lying down, his legs tucked under like a big dog. That was one of Beth's favorite times. She'd sit with her back against his and chatter on about what had happened in her day. He was, without doubt, her best friend.

Then one afternoon in late November, Beth came home to see the veterinarian's truck parked by Whoop's barn. She raced over to see the doctor examining Whoop. Ann had a worried expression on her face.

"Is he sick?"

"Hi, Beth. No, he's just a little off. When I rode him earlier this week he was slightly lame. I gave him a few days off and tried again this morning, but he seems a little worse. Dr. Smiler is just checking him out."

"I can't see anything wrong. He's a little off at the trot. Rest him another week, and if he's still lame, give me a call. With competent help like this young lady around, I'm sure he'll be doing better," said Dr. Smiler.

Still when the doctor left, Whoop looked at Beth and seemed a little sad.

Beth spent every afternoon with Whoop, grooming him, talking to him, and sometimes just sitting next to him. He seemed to be spending more time lying down than before, and she'd sit with him.

The new baby was quieting down. But Beth's feelings of irritation at the baby were minor compared to her worry for Whoop.

Ann was getting more worried, too. The vet came back out for another look, then another. Finally, he decided Whoop had sore front feet or hooves. It was a serious disease known as laminitis.

He prescribed all sorts of pills for Whoop to take. At first Ann would just break them up and put them in Whoop's food, but then he stopped eating his food. Then she mixed the pills up in hot water and molasses, and actually squirted it into his mouth like a huge shot without a needle.

Whoop seemed more and more depressed. He was no

longer out in the paddock when Beth came home from school. She'd find him standing or lying forlornly in the aisleway of the barn. His hooves were warm to the touch even when it was cold and snowy outside.

Beth would stand quietly holding Whoop's lead line when the vet would come to check on him, lifting his feet, tapping them.

After almost a dozen visits, Ann asked Dr. Smiler, "Isn't there anything more that can be done?" Her voice cracked slightly. Beth was very, very scared.

Ann had a dump truck deliver sand to the front of the barn. With a tractor she spread a layer inside the barn and in front of the door to give Whoop extra support for his feet.

The blacksmith came and put a special pair of shoes on Whoop's front feet. "It's like he has a toothache in his hoof," he explained to Ann and Beth. "A horse's hoof is like a fingernail, and this is like a blister growing behind it and pushing out the nail. If it separates, no one can help him."

"You mean he'll die?" asked Beth horrified.

"It means that it may hurt too much, and he's been too good a friend to want him to always be hurting. But we'll see. I'm not giving up on him yet," Ann said.

Ann tried all sorts of remedies that the vet suggested and that she heard about from others.

Beth told her mother and father about Whoop, and

they worried with her.

Nothing seemed to help. Whoop looked sadder and more dejected than ever.

School recessed for the holiday break and Beth spent even more time with Whoop.

Her mom and dad sat down with her one night and explained to her that sometimes when animals are sick nothing more can be done for them, and to be kind they had to be put to sleep. She knew they were talking about Whoop, but she couldn't listen.

At the stable where she had her riding lessons, her instructor told the young riders about a legend that all animals can talk at midnight on Christmas Eve. On that magical night all animals have special powers.

Beth asked Ann about it, and she smiled and said it was a very special time and anything might happen. Meanwhile, the vet visited again and shook his head and said there was nothing more he could do. "You're going to have to make a decision soon," he told Ann. She nodded, but told him not until the holidays were over. He shrugged and drove off.

Beth made a very special gift for Whoop, sewing a Christmas stocking and filling it with apples, pears and carrots. All were his favorites. Whoop seemed increasingly uninterested in everything around him even Beth and Ann.

On Christmas Eve, Beth went to church with her parents and baby brother—he naturally cried most of the time. When they went home, she went to bed, her parents winking at her and teasing that Santa would be coming soon.

Secretly, Beth set her alarm clock for 11:30 p.m. and put it under her pillow. The house was quiet when it jangled in her ear. She got up, dressed quickly in the dark and silently tiptoed out of the house carrying the stocking she had made for Whoop.

He was there lying on his side his legs stretched out, a night light that Ann had installed casting a feeble glow over the barn.

"Whoop, it's me. It's almost midnight on Christmas. Please tell me what's wrong. You've got to get better. You are my best friend. I love you."

Whoop sighed and whickered softly, then rolled into a tucked position.

Beth settled in next to him feeling suddenly sleepy until she felt him grow tense. She jumped to her feet as he hoisted himself up and whickered a greeting. A white horse she had never seen before nuzzled him, and he nuzzled her back, then rubbed his neck against hers. They seemed to stand together forever, nickering back and forth.

"Whoop, who is that?"

"I'm Seline," said the beautiful white horse. "I'm here to help Whoop. He has been in great pain."

"Is he going to die?" Beth asked.

"That's up to Whoop. He can get better if he chooses to. He knows now, I'm always around him. I'll be here waiting."

Then, the white horse was gone.

Beth stood there uncertain, convinced what she'd seen was real, but maybe it was not. Whoop was lying tucked on the ground again.

She knelt next to him and put her arms around his neck. "Oh, Whoop, I love you so much. Please don't die. I know someday you will, but not now . . . not yet. Ann and I both need you."

"I'll try," came the whispered answer.

Beth started crying and Whoop got up slowly, careful not to hurt the little girl. "I love you, too," he whispered softly.

After a long time, Beth slipped out of the barn and walked back to the house, leaving footprints in the fresh snow that had fallen during what was now a starry night.

The next morning, she rushed out to the barn, and Whoop pranced out to greet her, cantering up and down in a snowy game of tag.

Ann noticed him through her kitchen window and came running out. Whoop galloped up to her, wheeled, snorted then pranced off.

Ann and Beth went into the barn. Whoop followed, stomping his feet, hungry for his breakfast. Ann had made him a special one, slicing up apples, pears and carrots to add to his grain.

He ate hungrily, then stood contentedly munching his hay.

Beth, in words that tumbled over one another, told her what had happened the previous night. Ann, smiling broadly, examined Whoop closely, feeling his front hooves and checking his pulse behind his forelegs. Everything felt normal.

Whoop, his eyes gentle, seemed more peaceful.

Beth told her story over breakfast with her family.

Over the next few days, Whoop improved steadily before their eyes.

The vet came out and shook his head in disbelief. "I thought you were a goner, old man."

Beth told him about what she had seen Christmas Eve at midnight. The doctor shook his head and smiled kindly in disbelief. "Well, that's real interesting," he said.

Then he stopped, a funny look on his face, and asked her to repeat the white horse's name.

"She called herself Seline," said Beth.

"Well, I'll be. You don't know this Ann, but Whoop used to be stabled with a white mare named Seline. They

had the same dam. That's mother," he explained to Beth. "They were crazy about each other. It was at least 15 or more years ago. Then you got Whoop, and Seline moved to another barn. I forgot about that. Seline died last spring. . . . That's crazy. Couldn't be. Are sure you didn't fall asleep out there young lady?"

Whoop snorted and shook his head, "No!" Beth, Ann and the vet looked at him. Beth and Ann started grinning and threw their arms around Whoop's neck.

The vet just shook his head, walked back to his truck and drove off. "Impossible," was the last thing Beth and Ann heard him say.

Both Beth and Ann swear Whoop quietly chuckled.

Beth still races off the bus in a hurry to check in with Whoop. But now she takes some time to play with her little brother, too. She's decided when he gets a little older she'll tell him a story about two horses who were brother and sister.

The End

Jane Briggs-Bunting is a professor of journalism at Oakland University. She has written for *People* and *Life* magazines and is a former staff writer for the *Detroit Free Press*. A Cleveland, Ohio, native, she fell in love with horses when she was seven years old. She lives in Oxford, Michigan, with her husband, Robert, an attorney, five cats, two dogs, three swans and, of course, Whoop for Joy.

Jon Buechel was the fashion artist for the *Detroit Free Press*. His sketches and whimsical drawings graced the pages of the newspaper for 43 years. He is retired, though he still does a weekly drawing entitled "Buechel's World" which appears Sundays in the *Free Press*. His drawings are collected by readers across the region. Born and raised in Center Line, Michigan, he still lives there with his wife of 45 years, Shirley. They have three grown daughters and two grandchildren.

Whoop for Joy is a 24-year-old retired race horse who lives on a farm in Oxford, Michigan. He was foaled in Florida to racing parents. In his six year career on the track, he won his only race at the Detroit Race Course on June 19, 1975. He retired from the track in 1978 and began his second career as a dressage and western competitor for a girl in Addison Township. When she grew up, fell in love and planned to marry, she sold Whoop, who was then 12 years old, to Jane Briggs-Bunting for the price of her wedding gown. He's been living on her farm in Oxford ever since. They saunter together down the gravel roads and country trails in the area.

Special thanks to Wallis Andersen and Robert Snell for their technical assistance, and to Wallis Andersen, again, and Mary Hoisington for their help in editing. Thanks, as well, to Carolyn Stevens for her insistence I write this book.